MAY 14 2009

WITHDRAWN FROM LIBRARY

J
958.1
BURGAN

AFGHANISTAN

Countries in CRISIS

MICHAEL BURGAN

Rourke Publishing

© 2009 Rourke Publishing LLC

All rights reserved. No part of this book may be reproduced or utilized in any form or by any means, electronic or mechanical including photocopying, recording, or by any information storage and retrieval system without permission in writing from the publisher.

www.rourkepublishing.com

PHOTO CREDITS: Sgt. Joe Belcher/courtesy of U.S. Army: p. 5; Bettmann/Corbis: p. 22; Jean Claude-Chapon/AFP/Getty Images: p. 31; Library of Congress: p. 17; Gene Corley/F.E.M.A: p. 32; Douglas E. Curran/AFP/Getty Images: p. 27; Department of Defense: p. 29; Getty Images: p. 30; Hulton Archive/Getty Images: pp. 15, 19; Hulton Deutsch Collection/Getty Images: p. 16; istockphoto.com: p. 11; Keystone/Getty Images: p. 21; Sgt. Frank Magni/ courtesy of U.S. Army: p. 37; Mai/Mai/Time Life Pictures/Getty Images: p. 25; Shai Marai/AFP/Getty Images: pp. 7, 36; Easi-Images/Jenny Matthews: pp. 12, 41; Yiannis Papadimitriou/istock: p. 10; Pfc. Mike Pryor/courtesy of U.S. Army: pp. 6, 38; Reuters/Corbis: p. 26; Reza/Getty Images: p. 39; Patrick Robert/Corbis: p. 34; Travel Ink/Getty Images: p. 9; Zaheerudin/Webistan/Corbis: p. 28.

Cover picture shows an Afghan policeman and U.S. soldier at a checkpoint near the ruined palace of Darlaman, Kabul, Afghanistan. (SHAH MARAI/AFP/Getty Images)

Produced for Rourke Publishing by Discovery Books
Editor: Gill Humphrey
Designer: Keith Williams
Map: Stefan Chabluk
Photo researcher: Rachel Tisdale

Library of Congress Cataloging-in-Publication Data

Burgan, Michael.
   Afghanistan / Michael Burgan.
      p. cm. -- (Countries in crisis)
   ISBN 978-1-60472-349-6
   1. Afghanistan--Juvenile literature. I. Title.
   DS351.5.B87 2009
   958.1--dc22

2008025

Printed in the USA

CONTENTS

Chapter 1: War Zone — 4

Chapter 2: Crossroads of Asia — 8

Chapter 3: Independence — 14

Chapter 4: The Soviets Arrive — 20

Chapter 5: Life Under the Taliban — 28

Chapter 6: The Violence Continues — 34

Timeline — 43

Afghanistan Fact File — 44

Glossary — 46

Further Information — 47

Index — 48

CHAPTER ONE

WAR ZONE

In June 2007, the people of Gereshk, Afghanistan, watched as workers built a new school. In nearby Lashkar Gah, new wells had recently been dug to provide clean water, and in another part of town, a new park was almost finished. All these building projects were paid for by the British government.

Great Britain, the United States, and other **democratic** nations had sent more than 50,000 soldiers to Afghanistan. Most of these countries belong to the **North Atlantic Treaty Organization (NATO)**. NATO countries also sent billions of dollars in aid. Their goal was to fight **terrorists** and rebels who wanted to destroy Afghanistan's new democratic government.

THE TALIBAN

The rebels were called the Taliban. This means *religious students* in Pashto, one of the languages spoken in Afghanistan. The Taliban once ruled Afghanistan. They limited the freedom of the people and strictly followed the teachings of the Islamic religion. The Taliban also supported a terrorist group called al-Qaeda. On September 11, 2001, members of al-Qaeda carried out four terrorist attacks in the United States that killed almost 3,000 people. In response, U.S. President George W. Bush assembled an international army

AFGHANISTAN

U.S. army troops drive through the village of Torkham in 2004. Tens of thousands of foreign troops serve in Afghanistan, trying to bring peace to the country.

to go to Afghanistan. Its aim was to capture al-Qaeda leaders and remove the Taliban from power.

The United States and its **allies** quickly defeated the Taliban and helped set up a democratic government in Afghanistan. But they did not catch all the al-Qaeda leaders or completely destroy the Taliban.

COUNTRIES IN CRISIS WAR ZONE

DECADES OF WAR

The people of Afghanistan are used to war. It has been part of their daily life for almost 30 years. Through most of the 1990s, Afghans fought a **civil war**. Members of different **ethnic** and religious groups clashed as they tried to gain power. The civil war followed a long war with the **Soviet Union**. The Soviets invaded Afghanistan in 1979. The Afghans fought for almost ten years before finally driving the Soviets out of the country.

By 2006, a growing number of Taliban were fighting NATO and Afghan government forces in different parts of the country. Al-Qaeda carried out attacks as well.

People try to live normal lives, but they know their country is still filled with danger. In Lashkar Gah,

Afghan soldiers question a man, while a U.S. soldier provides security from his vehicle. After the removal of the Taliban in 2001, the new Afghan National Army was created with help from NATO forces.

6

AFGHANISTAN

WAR AND THE INNOCENT

> "A lot of innocent women, children and men die during every bombing campaign. This doesn't happen just once...people die, get injured or lose their houses. It happens all the time."
>
> *A doctor at Bost Hospital in Lashkar Gah, speaking in November 2007.*

where the new park was built, a bomb exploded in October 2007. It killed four people and wounded seven others. Many Afghans wonder when their country will finally see peace.

In June 2007, the Taliban planted the bomb that destroyed this police bus in the Afghan capital of Kabul. In recent years, the Taliban has increased its attacks across Afghanistan.

CHAPTER TWO

CROSSROADS OF ASIA

Afghanistan is in Central Asia. It is about the size of New Mexico and Arizona combined. Almost 32 million people live in Afghanistan. The nation is completely surrounded by land. Its neighbors are Pakistan to the south and east, Iran to the west, and Turkmenistan, Uzbekistan, and Tajikistan to the

WHERE IS AFGHANISTAN?

AFGHANISTAN is in Central Asia

AFGHANISTAN

The mountains of the Hindu Kush rise above Bamiyan, in central Afghanistan. Melting snow on the peaks provides water for most of the country's rivers.

north. A tiny part of Afghanistan in the northeast touches the border of China.

The Afghans live in a land dominated by rugged mountains, particularly the Hindu Kush. In the western part of Afghanistan, deserts cover much of the land. Still, in some mountain valleys the land is good for raising crops and animals. Part of Afghanistan is in an area of land called the steppe. The land is flat and covered with grass. People there tend to be

9

COUNTRIES IN CRISIS CROSSROADS OF ASIA

With the conquests of Alexander the Great, shown here on horseback, Afghanistan became part of a huge Greek empire.

nomads that move from place to place, looking for grass for their animals. Today, nomadic life is slowly disappearing in Afghanistan.

The weather in Afghanistan can be extreme. In winter, strong snowstorms hit the eastern mountains. In the summer, the desert regions can see the temperature go over 120°F (49°C). Most of the country receives little snow or rain.

SETTLERS AND INVADERS

The first humans came to Afghanistan more than 30,000 years ago. About 9,000 years ago, the early Afghans began

AFGHANISTAN

Afghans have a long history of making wool rugs by hand. Most have colorful designs, like this one, but modern rugs sometimes show scenes of battle from Afghanistan's recent wars.

farming in the region. People from Central Asia called the Indo-Iranians entered Afghanistan about 4,000 years ago. Over the centuries, other people followed them. In 330 BC a Greek general named Alexander the Great defeated the Persians. Afghanistan became part of a new empire that stretched from southern Europe and Egypt to western India.

The foreign invasions did not end with the Greeks. People from India ruled southern Afghanistan for several decades. They brought the religion called **Buddhism**. In the 2nd century BC the Kushan Empire developed. Under Kushan rule, Afghanistan became a key part of the Silk Road. This trade route linked China with the Middle East and Europe. The Afghan cities of Balkh (Bactra) and Bagram were important trading sites on the Silk Road.

11

COUNTRIES IN CRISIS CROSSROADS OF ASIA

Muslims worship in mosques like the Blue Mosque in Mazar-i-Sharif. Skilled Afghan artists of the past used tile and stone to build many beautiful mosques and other buildings.

Archaeologists have found goods from China, Rome, Egypt, and India buried in Bagram.

ARABS, TURKS, AND MONGOLS

In 632, followers of an Arab religious leader named Muhammad began to attack neighboring lands. By 651, these followers of Islam had taken control of Afghanistan. Most Afghans

AFGHANISTAN

ISLAM

Muhammad was the founder of Islam. He said the God of the Jews and Christians had chosen him to receive messages. He would be the last of God's messengers on Earth, and Islam was the one true religion. Over time, Islam split into two major groups, Sunni and Shiite. The split was over which leaders Muslims should follow after Muhammad's death. Today, most Arabs and Afghans are Sunni. Iranians and some Arabs and Afghans are Shiite. A branch of Shiite Islam is called Ismaili. A small number of these Muslims also live in Afghanistan.

became **Muslims**, though a Persian influence remained.

Near the end of the 10th century, the Turks of Central Asia invaded Afghanistan. Then the Mongols of Central Asia stormed through the region. They created the largest land-based empire of all time.

By the early 1700s, Afghans could trace their roots to the many different foreigners who had ruled them. Persian, Arabic, and Turkic languages were spoken. Despite foreign rule, the Afghan tribes had some independence. But they wanted even more, and they soon won it.

CHAPTER THREE

INDEPENDENCE

In 1709, some Pashtun tribes rebelled against the Safavids, or Persian rulers, in the south and west of the country. They drove out the Persians and took control of parts of Iran. Other Pashtun tribes also rebelled. In 1747, a Pashtun named Ahmad Shah came to power. He created an independent nation that soon took over neighboring lands. Under his rule Afghanistan stretched from what is now eastern Iran through Pakistan and into India.

Ahmad Shah died in 1772. After his death, his son Timur ruled. When he died, his sons fought for control of the country. Within the country, different branches, or clans of the Durrani

This portrait of Dost Muhammad shows him around the time of the First Anglo-Afghan War.

FATHER OF HIS COUNTRY

Ahmad Shah Durrani (1722-1772) was also known as the father of Afghanistan. He took the name Durr-i-Durrani (*pearl of pearls*), and the tribe became known as the Durrani. It provided all of Afghanistan's rulers until 1978. Ahmad Shah was a strong believer in Islam. He was also known as a great general and a wise ruler.

14

AFGHANISTAN

tribe ruled their own areas. Finally, in 1826 Dost Muhammad came to power. He reunited the clans and helped bring peace to Afghanistan.

THE EUROPEANS ARRIVE

By this time, new outsiders had

COUNTRIES IN CRISIS INDEPENDENCE

taken an interest in the region. Great Britain now controlled large parts of India. It wanted to spread its influence into Afghanistan. Russia also had gained influence in Persia. It had taken control of steppe land north of Afghanistan. Great Britain and Russia saw each other as rivals in this part of the world.

The British supported a grandson of Ahmad Shah to become ruler of Afghanistan, and in 1839 they sent 21,000 troops into the country. The British were soon in control, but in 1841 Pashtun tribes began to rebel. British troops left Kabul but were attacked along the way. This was

As part of the rivalry between Britain and Russia, Russia sent money to Afghanistan so it could build these cannons. The British captured the guns in 1879.

AFGHANISTAN

THE KHYBER PASS

A pass is a gap in a mountain range that lets people travel from one side to the other. The most famous pass in Afghanistan is the Khyber Pass. It cuts through the Hindu Kush, linking Kabul with Peshawar, Pakistan. The pass has been used for several thousand years. During the 19th century, the British used the Khyber Pass to send troops into and out of Afghanistan. During the First Anglo-Afghan War, the Afghans attacked British troops traveling through the pass.

Camels, horses, and people travel through the Khyber Pass. The fort on the top of the mountain was captured by the British during the Second Anglo-Afghan War.

the First **Anglo**-Afghan War.

MORE WARS

When the British left, Dost Muhammad returned to power and ruled for 20 more years. After his death in 1863, Afghanistan again faced civil war. The British supported Dost Muhammad's son, Sher Ali. He finally emerged as the leader in 1868. Still, the British wanted more control in

COUNTRIES IN CRISIS INDEPENDENCE

> ### THE NEED TO UNITE
>
> "The first and most important advice that I can give to my successors [rulers that come later] and people to make Afghanistan into a great kingdom is to impress upon their minds the value of unity; unity, and unity alone, can make it into a great power."
>
> *Abdur Rahman Khan*

Afghanistan. In 1878, they sent troops into the country, sparking the Second Anglo-Afghan War. The British won the war and chose the new leader of Afghanistan, Abdur Rahman Khan.

Abdur Rahman was a brutal ruler. However, he tried to create a modern government, with departments for such things as education, trade, and justice.

Abdur Rahman's son, Habibullah, was not as cruel as his father. He tried to turn a country of nomads and tribal chiefs into a modern nation. He improved schooling and built roads, hospitals, and factories. Afghan leaders also pushed the idea that Afghanistan was a distinct nation that should rule itself. In 1919, Habibullah's son Amanullah launched the Third Anglo-Afghan War. This time the British were not willing to fight. The war ended quickly with an Afghan victory. The British agreed to give Afghanistan complete

AFGHANISTAN

During the 1920s, King Amanullah Khan (center, saluting) visited Germany on a tour of European nations. Amanullah ruled Afghanistan from 1919 to 1929.

independence and Amanullah became Afghanistan's leader.

CHAPTER FOUR

THE SOVIETS ARRIVE

During the 1920s Afghanistan's **communist** neighbor the Soviet Union tried to limit Islam in their Central Asian lands. Even though the Soviets opposed Islam and other religions, the Afghan government sometimes turned to them for help. Starting in the 1950s, the two countries began to trade with each other.

By the 1950s, the Soviet Union and the United States were the world's two most powerful countries. They were locked in a battle to win allies and influence foreign governments, but they did not want to go to war with each other. This struggle was called the Cold War. U.S. leaders did not want Afghanistan to become too friendly with the Soviet Union. The United States also sent money to the Afghans.

COMMUNISM IN AFGHANISTAN

During the 1950s and 1960s, thousands of young Afghans learned about communism. Some of them thought it could improve their country. Most people were still poor farmers, and had no say in how the government was run.

In 1964, King Zahir approved changes to the government. These changes brought greater democracy, but some Afghan communists wanted more change. Other Afghans called **Islamists** did not like the changes. They thought Islamic

AFGHANISTAN

King Zahir Shah took the throne in 1933 and ruled for 40 years. During the last years of his rule, more women in Kabul attended school than ever before.

teachings should influence both the government and society.

In 1973, Muhammad Daoud seized power from King Zahir.

COUNTRIES IN CRISIS THE SOVIETS ARRIVE

Some Afghan communists supported this new government. But Daoud did not give them a large role in his government. In 1978, Afghan communists took control of the government, with help from the Soviet Union. They arrested people who opposed communism and murdered Islamists. In the countryside, some tribal leaders rebelled. Others took their tribes into Pakistan where they set up camps to train as **guerrillas**.

AFGHANISTAN

In January 1980, Soviet tanks and trucks roll into Afghanistan. Within a few years, the Soviets had more than 100,000 troops in the country.

THE SOVIET INVASION

The Soviet Union wanted a communist government in Afghanistan, but it disliked the events taking place there. They decided to invade Afghanistan and set up a government they could control themselves.

The Soviet invasion began on December 25, 1979. Hundreds of Soviet tanks and thousands of soldiers headed for Kabul and soon controlled the capital. The invasion angered U.S. president Jimmy Carter and other democratic leaders. But the United States was not willing to take direct military action. Instead, it began to send money and weapons to Pakistan. The Pakistanis then gave the aid to the Afghans living in their country and along the border. The United States also secretly gave some weapons directly to the Afghan rebels.

COUNTRIES IN CRISIS THE SOVIETS ARRIVE

A DANGEROUS INVASION

> If the Soviets. . .maintain their dominance over Afghanistan and then extend their control. . .the stable. . .and peaceful balance of the entire world will be changed. This would threaten the security of all nations including, of course, the United States, our allies, and our friends.

President Jimmy Carter, after the Soviet invasion of Afghanistan.

Afghans of different tribes fought the Soviets. They were called **mujahideen**. This Arabic word means *those who fight jihad.*

A *jihad* is a war, particularly against non-Muslims. The mujahideen wanted to end communism in Afghanistan.

EFFECTS OF THE SOVIET-AFGHAN WAR

By most counts, almost 2 million Afghans were killed during the war with the Soviet Union. Another 5 million or so became **refugees**. They fled from Afghanistan to Iran, Pakistan, and other countries. On the Soviet side, more than 50,000 troops were killed or wounded during the war.

AFGHANISTAN

A mujahideen fires a Stinger missile. As they battled the Soviets, the Afghans received these and other modern weapons from the United States.

A CIVIL WAR

Peace, however, did not come to Afghanistan. Some Afghans still wanted a communist government, and the Soviets gave them weapons and money. These Afghans battled the mujahideen, who were split into several different groups. Most were based on ethnic background, such as Pashtun, Uzbek, or Tajik. Most mujahideen stayed united long enough to defeat the Afghan government in 1992. But soon they were fighting each other.

Some rebels wanted to create an Islamic state. Muslims from other countries came to Afghanistan to help achieve this goal. The Soviet-Afghan war dragged on through the 1980s. The Soviets finally realized they could not defeat the rebels, and left Afghanistan in 1989.

COUNTRIES IN CRISIS THE SOVIETS ARRIVE

In 1989, a Soviet soldier prepares to go home after serving in Afghanistan. During the war, the Soviet Union controlled major cities, while the mujahideen controlled the countryside.

AFGHANISTAN

In 1994, a new group, called the Taliban, entered the conflict. These religious students and teachers were mostly Pashtun, from Afghanistan and Pakistan. The Taliban received money from Islamists in Pakistan and Saudi Arabia. More Afghans began to support the Taliban, since they were bringing order to the country. By 1998, the Taliban controlled almost all of Afghanistan.

In April 1992, a Kabul resident examines damaged carpets after a battle between rival groups of mujahideen. The fighting broke out the same day the former Afghan government gave up its rule.

CHAPTER FIVE

LIFE UNDER THE TALIBAN

The leader of the Taliban was **Mullah** Mohammad Omar. Under him, the Taliban imposed a strict version of Islamic law to rule Afghanistan. Women were not allowed to work outside the home and girls were not allowed to go to school. In public, women had to wear a burka. This long robe covered their entire body. Other Taliban laws forced men to go to religious services at mosques. Afghans were also forbidden to watch TV, listen to music, fly kites, or play soccer.

A teacher gives one of her last lessons. After taking power, the Taliban closed private schools and forbade girls over eight years old from attending public schools.

AFGHANISTAN

OSAMA BIN LADEN

Born in Syria, Osama bin Laden (1957-) came from a wealthy Saudi Arabian family. He inherited hundreds of millions of dollars and used some of this money to fund the Afghan mujahideen against the Soviet Union. Bin Laden wanted to spread his version of Islam around the world. To do this, he attacked countries that he thought weakened Islam. At the top of his list was the United States.

Many Afghans did not like the new laws. The Uzbeks, Tajiks, Hazara, and others who opposed the Taliban, united to form the Northern Alliance. They battled the Taliban for control of the country.

Osama bin Laden used some of his money to help the Afghan mujahideen fight the Soviet Union. He then used his wealth to fund terrorism.

TEACHING TERRORISM

To fight the Northern Alliance, the Taliban relied on help from foreigners. Some Arabs and Pakistanis supported the Taliban's extreme form of Islam. One of the most important Arabs was Osama bin Laden. He had fought against

COUNTRIES IN CRISIS LIFE UNDER THE TALIBAN

the Soviets and then left the country to plan terrorist attacks on the United States and other democratic nations. Bin Laden returned to Afghanistan in 1996. He gave money to the Taliban and helped train its soldiers.

In return for bin Laden's help, Mullah Omar let him set up terrorist training camps where thousands of non-Afghan Muslims learned how to fight. Some trained to become suicide bombers. They would blow themselves up so they could kill others at the same time. Bin Laden and his terrorists were known as al-Qaeda.

In 1998, some al-Qaeda terrorists bombed two U.S. **embassies** in Africa killing more than 200 people. The next

Terrorists train in Afghanistan. This image comes from a video al-Qaeda made to recruit more fighters.

AFGHANISTAN

DESTROYING HISTORY

The Taliban believed Islam was the only true religion. They opposed other religions. In March, the world was shocked to see the Taliban destroy a great piece of Afghan history in the name of religion. For almost 1,500 years, two stone statues of the Buddha stood near a cliff in Bamiyan. Over the course of two weeks, the Taliban blew up the statues. Today, archaeologists are searching for a third giant Buddha that still may exist within the cliffs.

One of the two ancient statues of Buddha before the Taliban blew it up in 2001. The two Bamiyan Buddhas were more than 100 feet (30.5 meters) tall.

year, the **United Nations (UN)** demanded that the Taliban give bin Laden to U.S. officials so he could face trial. Mullah Omar refused.

Over the next few years, most countries refused to deal with the Afghanistan government.

COUNTRIES IN CRISIS LIFE UNDER THE TALIBAN

They opposed its harsh rule and support of terrorism. The countries hoped to force the Taliban to turn over bin Laden and shut down the terrorist camps. Still, the Taliban ignored these demands.

THE SEPTEMBER 11 ATTACKS

On the morning of September 11, 2001, Americans watched with horror as two airplanes flew into the Twin Towers of New York City's World Trade Center. Another plane

A worker goes through the wreckage of the New York City World Trade Center after the September 11, 2001 terrorist attack.

AFGHANISTAN

A CALL FOR ACTION

> The United States respects the people of Afghanistan...but we condemn the Taliban regime. The Taliban must act, and act immediately. They will hand over the terrorists, or they will share in their fate.
>
> *President George W. Bush, in a speech to the American public, September 20, 2001.*

flew into the Pentagon in Washington D.C. A fourth plane crashed in Pennsylvania.

The four planes had been taken over by al-Qaeda terrorists. Their attacks killed almost 3,000 people. Some of the terrorists had trained in Afghanistan.

President George W. Bush demanded that the Taliban turn over bin Laden and shut down all the terrorist camps. If the Taliban refused, the United States and its allies would attack Afghanistan. They would hunt down bin Laden and force the Taliban out of power. In Afghanistan, Mullah Omar refused Bush's demands.

He said the United States tried to control Islamic countries and that the Taliban had to resist, even if it meant Afghans would be killed. Once again, Afghans prepared for war.

CHAPTER SIX

THE VIOLENCE CONTINUES

In October 2001, the United States and its allies began bombing Taliban targets in Afghanistan. The bombing raids destroyed Taliban missiles and airfields. Within a few weeks, the Northern Alliance was moving southward. Taliban fighters fled south, where they had the strongest support. But promises of U.S.

A little more than a month after the United States began bombing Afghanistan, these Taliban troops surrender. The Taliban had already lost control of Kabul and other major cities.

AFGHANISTAN

money led some Pashtun tribes to turn against the Taliban. In early December 2001, Mullah Omar surrendered. The Americans and their allies began destroying al-Qaeda camps and searching for Osama bin Laden. However, most al-Qaeda members had already fled to the mountains that border Afghanistan and Pakistan.

REBUILDING AFGHANISTAN

By the end of 2001, Afghanistan had a new government led by Hamid Karzai. The new Afghan government had to rebuild cities destroyed by decades of war. It also hoped to end the bad feelings between different ethnic and religious groups, to restore rights to women, and to build a united country.

Foreign governments sent billions of dollars in aid to help rebuild the country. In 2004, the people of Afghanistan had the first election in their history to choose their own ruler. Karzai was elected president for five years. He knew his job would be hard, but he hoped Afghans would keep working together to build a better country.

NEW TROUBLES

Afghanistan, however, still faced death and destruction. Through 2005 and 2006, several thousand Taliban and al-Qaeda fighters returned. Some Afghans believed

35

COUNTRIES IN CRISIS **THE VIOLENCE CONTINUES**

A PROUD PEOPLE

" We have held this country together after so much destruction, because. . .there was a deeply rooted nation of history and proud people who loved their country.

Hamid Karzai, speaking in 2005. "

Harmid Karzai speaks shortly before winning Afghanistan's first presidential election. Karzai, a Pashtun, was popular with some mujahideen because he helped fight the Soviet Union.

that Iran was providing bombs to terrorists in Afghanistan.

The Taliban and al-Qaeda tried to attack U.S. and NATO forces in Afghanistan. They planted hidden bombs along roads and used suicide bombers to kill Afghan police and soldiers, and **civilians**

AFGHANISTAN

WOMEN AFTER THE TALIBAN

The end of the Taliban brought changes for Afghan women. They were not required to wear burkas, though many still did. They could work outside of the home. The government also said at least one-quarter of its new lawmakers had to be women. But old ideas about women did not go away. Girls were still less likely to be allowed to go to schools. Many families still chose the person their daughters would marry.

Women wearing burkas register to vote in Kandahar in 2004.

COUNTRIES IN CRISIS THE VIOLENCE CONTINUES

working for the government or the peacekeepers.

The violence got even worse in 2007. About 5,000 people were killed that year, the most since 2001. The Taliban took control of several towns. At times, NATO and U.S. troops drove them out and killed important military leaders. But after they left, the Taliban often returned. In the north, tribal leaders and **warlords** began to collect weapons. They were not sure the Karzai government could keep

A U.S. soldier stands guard while other troops search a bike shop. NATO forces often look for people who might support the Taliban or al-Qaeda.

THE POPPY PROBLEM

Afghanistan produces almost all of the world's opium poppies. Farmers can make more money growing this flower than from other crops. But the opium and heroin produced from them can cause misery and death to drug users. And the money earned from the trade often goes to the Taliban or other rebels. The U.S. government and NATO are working hard to destroy poppy fields, but they also have to rebuild roads and canals to make it easier for Afghan farmers to grow other crops.

An Afghan farmer walks through a poppy field. Some U.S. officials have asked Afghan leaders to kill the poppies by spraying them with harmful chemicals.

COUNTRIES IN CRISIS THE VIOLENCE CONTINUES

> **LISTEN TO THE LEADERS**
>
> "For the past 25 years, we have been at war and we have a lot of rivalries and enemies here. And [the foreign troops] became part of it by relying only on one source. If these Americans had acted on the advice of our district administrator, the police chief, or the tribal elders, then they would have rebuilt Afghanistan by now."
>
> *Tribal leader Mullah Haji Habibullah, speaking to Radio Free Europe/Radio Liberty in 2007.*

order and wanted to be prepared if a new civil war broke out. Guns also offered protection against drug lords. Drug lords had became rich selling opium and wanted to protect their business at any cost.

Some tribal leaders in small villages felt no one listened to their concerns. They became angry when U.S. or NATO attacks accidentally killed civilians. But the Taliban and al-Qaeda chose to live near civilians, hoping the Americans wouldn't attack if innocent people were nearby.

THE FUTURE OF AFGHANISTAN

As 2008 began, the United States

Since the end of Taliban rule, Afghan girls of all ages can now go to school. Some women, however, still face limits on what they can do in public.

AFGHANISTAN

COUNTRIES IN CRISIS THE VIOLENCE CONTINUES

made plans to send an extra 3,200 troops to Afghanistan. Afghans still struggle to rebuild their cities, and the continuous fighting makes it hard for the UN and other groups to get aid to the poor. The troubles also keep several million children from going to school. Without education these children will not get good jobs, and some teenage boys may be tempted to fight for the Taliban or al-Qaeda, to earn money.

Afghanistan remains one of the poorest countries in the world. The U.S. and its allies still send aid to Afghanistan. They want to build a strong democratic government there. They do not want the country to be controlled by the Taliban or other terrorist groups. The Afghan people just hope that peace will come to their country.

REFUGEES

When the Taliban was forced from power, Afghan refugees began to return to their homeland. Since 2002, almost 4 million Afghans have come home. But in 2008, over 2 million refugees still lived in Iran and Pakistan. Many had been born in those countries, where their families have lived for 20 years or more.

TIMELINE

BC
- **ca. 2000** Indo-Iranians settle in Afghanistan.
- **330** Greek general Alexander the Great takes over Persian Empire, including Afghanistan.
- **ca. 135** Kushans settle in the region and begin to build an empire.

AD
- **651** Arabs conquer Afghanistan and introduce the religion of Islam.
- **ca. 1220** The Mongols begin their conquest of Central Asia, including Afghanistan.
- **1747** Ahmad Shah creates an independent Afghan kingdom.
- **1826** Rise of Dost Muhammad, who unites warring Afghan clans.
- **1839** Great Britain sends troops into Afghanistan, seeking to influence the government there.
- **1841** Pashtun tribes rebel against the British, sparking the First Anglo-Afghan War.
- **1878** British troops return, leading to the Second Anglo-Afghan War, which the British win.
- **1919** Amanullah Khan launches Third Anglo-Afghan War leading to full Afghan independence.
- **1964** King Zahir accepts changes to the government that lead to greater democracy.
- **1973** The Afghan monarchy ends.
- **1978** Communists take control of the Afghan government.
- **1979** The Soviet Union invades Afghanistan.
- **1989** Soviet troops leave Afghanistan.
- **1992** Mujahideen take control of the government but begin fighting with each other.
- **1994** The Taliban enters the battle to control Afghanistan.
- **1998** The Taliban controls most of Afghanistan and has close relations with Osama bin Laden.
- **2001** Al-Qaeda terrorists launch attacks on the United States; U.S. and international troops come to Afghanistan to force the Taliban from power.
- **2004** Harmid Karzai is elected president of a democratic Afghanistan.
- **2005** Taliban and al-Qaeda forces fight U.S. and allied troops still in Afghanistan.
- **2008** The United States sends more troops to Afghanistan, as violence continues.

FACT FILE

AFGHANISTAN

GEOGRAPHY

Area: 636,000 square miles (1.65 million sq. km.)

Borders: China, Iran, Pakistan, Tajikistan, Turkmenistan, Uzbekistan

Terrain: Mostly rugged mountains with plains in the north and southwest

Highest point: Nowshak 24,550 feet (7,485 meters)

Resources: Natural gas, petroleum, coal, copper, iron ore, salt, lead, zinc, salt, precious and semiprecious stones

Major rivers: Amu Darya, Harirud, Helmand, Kabul

SOCIETY

Population (2007): 31,889,923

Ethnic groups: Pashtun, Tajik, Hazara, Uzbek, Aimak, Turkmen, Baloch,

Languages: Afghan Persian or Dari, Pashto, Turkic languages (mainly Uzbek and Turkmen), other minor languages, much bilingualism   **Literacy:** 28.1%

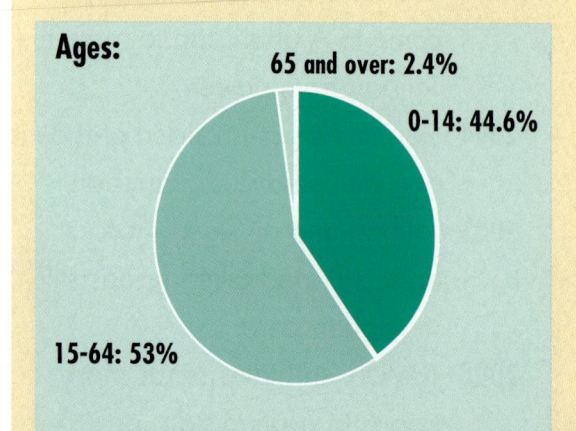

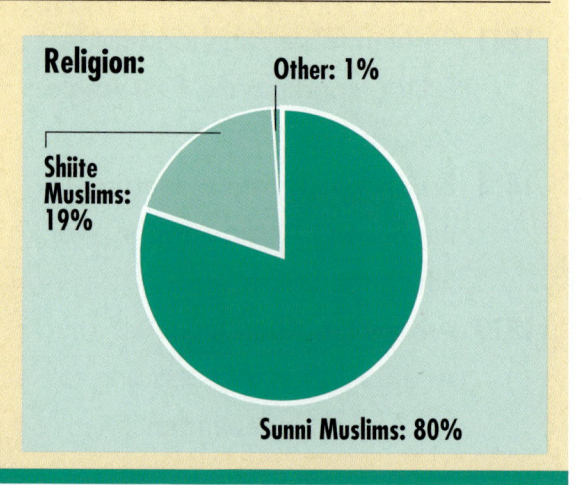

Ages:
- 0-14: 44.6%
- 15-64: 53%
- 65 and over: 2.4%

Religion:
- Sunni Muslims: 80%
- Shiite Muslims: 19%
- Other: 1%

44

GOVERNMENT

Type: Islamic republic

Capital: Kabul   **Provinces**: 34

Independence: August 19, 1919 (from British control)

Law: Mixed civil and Shari'a law

Vote: Universal—18 years of age

System: President (chief of state and head of government) Vice President, National Assembly, 249 seats (elected for 5-year term)

ECONOMY

Currency: afghani

Labor force (2004): 15 million

Total value of goods and services (2006): $32.4 billion

Poverty (2003): 53% of the population below poverty line

Main industries: opium, wheat, fruits, nuts, wool, mutton, sheep skins, carpets   **Foreign debt (2004/5):** over $749 billion + over $10 billion in disputed Russian claims

Sectors of industry (2007)
- industry 24%
- agriculture (excluding opium) 38%
- services 38%

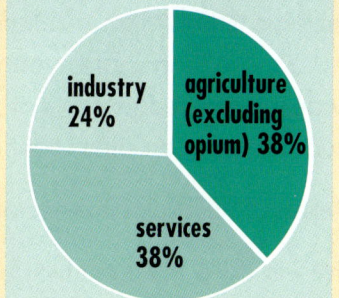

COMMUNICATIONS AND MEDIA

Telephones (2005): 280,000 lines; 2.52 million mobile (2006)

Internet users (2006): 535,000   **TV stations:** 20 stations (1 state-run station, 7 privately-owned stations)   **Newspapers:** several daily papers and two weeklies

Radio: Radio Afghanistan—state-run, 3 private stations/networks

Airports: 46 (only 12 with paved runways)

Railroads: almost none   **Roads:** 21,612 miles (34,782 km)

MILITARY

Branches: Army, air force

Service: military service at age 22 for a 4-year term

GLOSSARY

allies (AL-ize): friendly countries that will support each other militarily

Anglo (AN-glow): relating to the English or English-speaking people

archaeologists (ar kee OL uh gists): scientists who study the remains left behind by ancient peoples

Buddhism (BOO-diz-uhm): a religion founded in India more than 2,500 years ago that is widely practiced in parts of Asia. Some Buddhists live on other continents too.

civilians (si-VIL-yuhns): citizens not in the military

civil war (SIV-il WOR): conflict between two or more groups inside the same country

communist (KOM-yuh-nist): a political system that calls for one party to control the government and for the government to own most property

democratic (dem-uh-KRAT-tik): having a form of government that allows the people to elect their own leaders

embassies (EM-buh-sees): the places where officials work and live while representing their government in other nations

ethnic (ETH-nik): people sharing the same origins, history, culture, and language

guerrillas (guh-RIL-uhs): small groups that take part in fighting larger forces or armies. They often make surprise raids on an invading enemy.

Islamists (ISS-lulm-ists): Muslims who believe in strictly following the Qu'ran and other Islamic teachings

mujahideen (moo-juh-hi-DEEN): an Arabic word meaning fighter or someone who struggles

Mullah (MUH-luh): a title of respect for some Islamic religious leaders

Muslims (MUHZ-luhms): followers of the religion of Islam

North Atlantic Treaty Organization (NATO): an organization of nations set up to help defend member countries if they are attacked. NATO sometimes sends troops to non-NATO countries like Afghanistan.

nomads (NOH-madz): people who move from place to place looking for food for themselves and their animals

refugees (ref-yuh-JEEZ): people who are forced to leave home because of war or other dangerous situations

Soviet Union (SOH-vee-et yoon-yuhn): a former federation of communist republics including Russia

terrorists (TER-ur-ists): people or organizations that use violence to bring about change

United Nations (UN) (yoo-NI-tid NAY-shuhns): an international organization set up to help promote peace

warlords (WOR-lords): local officials or tribal leaders who command private armies

FURTHER INFORMATION

WEBSITES

Afghanistan Online
http://www.afghan-web.com/
This site has information on Afghan culture, history, politics, languages, sports, and much more.

BBC News – Afghanistan's Future
http://news.bbc.co.uk/2/hi/in_depth/south_asia/2004/afghanistan/default.stm
This site has the latest news stories as well as video, and audio reports, and special news stories on the lives of ordinary Afghans.

CIA World Factbook – Afghanistan
https://www.cia.gov/library/publications/the-world-factbook/geos/af.html
The site has lots of facts and statistics on Afghanistan.

Islamic Republic of Afghanistan – Office of the President
http://www.president.gov.af/
The site has information on the government of Afghanistan and its president, Hamid Karzai.

NATO International Assistance Force (Afghanistan)
http://www.nato.int/isaf/index.html
This site has lots of information and news stories on the work of the International Security Assistance Force.

UN High Commissioner for Refugees – Afghanistan
http://www.unhcr.org/cgi-bin/texis/vtx/country?iso=afg
The site has information on the work of the UN Refugee Agency in Afghanistan.

BOOKS

September 11. Mary Englar, Minneapolis: Compass Point Books, 2007.

Afghanistan. 2nd ed. Jeffrey A. Gritzner, New York: Chelsea House Publishers, 2007.

Afghanistan. Charles Piddock, Milwaukee: World Almanac Press, 2007.

Life Under the Taliban. Gail B. Stewart, San Diego: Lucent Books, 2005.

Islam. Philip Wilkinson, New York: Dorling Kindersley, 2005.

Harmid Karzai: President of Afghanistan. Philip Wolny, New York: Rosen Publishing Group, 2007.

Hideouts and Training Camps (Fighting Terrorism series). David Baker, Florida: Rourke Publishing, 2006.

INDEX

Afghan tribes and leaders, 13, 14, 22, 24, 25, 27, 29, 35, 38, 40
Afghanistan, rebuilding of, 4, 35, 42
Afghanistan, war in, 35-42
Alexander the Great, 10, 11
al-Qaeda, 4, 5, 6, 30, 33, 35, 36, 38, 40, 42
Anglo-Afghan Wars, 16, 17-18,

Bamiyan Buddhas, 31
bin-Laden, Osama, 29-30, 32, 33, 35
Britain, 4, 15, 16, 17, 18,
Buddhism, 11
Bush, George W., (U.S. president), 4, 33

Carter, Jimmy (U.S. president), 23, 24
civil wars, 6, 17, 25, 26
Cold War, the, 20
communism, 20, 22, 23, 24, 25

Daoud, Muhammad, 21
drug lords, 40
Durrani, Ahmad Shah, 14

education, 42
elections (2004), 35, 37

Iran, 24, 35
Islam, 12-13,
Islamic law, 28
Islamists, 20-21, 22, 25, 27

Karzai, Hamid, 35, 36, 38
Khan, Abdur Rahman, 18
Khan, Amanullah, 18-19
Khan, Habibullah, 18
Khyber Pass, 17

Mongols, 13
Muhammad, Dost, 14, 15, 17
mujahideen, 24, 25, 26, 27, 29

NATO, 4, 6, 36, 38, 39, 40
nomads, 10
Northern Alliance, 29, 34

Omar, Mullah Mohammad, 28, 30, 31, 33, 35
opium poppies, 39, 40

Pakistan, 22, 23, 24, 27, 29, 35
Persians, 11, 13, 14

refugees, 24, 42
Russia, 16

Saudi Arabia, 27
September 11, 2001 terrorist attacks, 4, 32-33
Shah, King Zahir, 20, 21
Silk Road, 11-12
Soviet-Afghan War, 24-25, 26
Soviet Union, 6, 20, 22, 23, 24, 25, 26

Taliban, 4, 5, 6, 7, 27-33, 34-39, 40, 42
terrorism, 4, 7, 29, 30, 32-33, 36,
terrorist training camps, 30, 32, 33, 35
Turks, 13

United Nations (UN), 31, 42
United States, 4, 5, 20, 23, 29, 30, 32-35, 36, 38, 39, 40, 42

women, 28, 35, 37, 40